This Orchard book
belongs to...

To Queen Lucy and Princess Tara, who both like being
read to sleep – P.B.

For my wonderful Grandparents. Nanny Sheila, who always
loved a game of Ludo with the family. And Grandad John, who
makes a cracking cup of tea! – L.E.A.

ORCHARD BOOKS
338 Euston Road, London NW1 3BH
Orchard Books Australia
Level 17/207 Kent Street, Sydney, NSW 2000

First published in 2014 by Orchard Books
First published in paperback in 2015

ISBN 978 1 40833 061 6

Text © Peter Bently 2014
Illustrations © Laura Ellen Anderson 2014

The rights of Peter Bently to be identified as the author
and of Laura Ellen Anderson to be identified as the illustrator
of this work have been asserted by them in accordance with
the Copyright, Designs and Patents Act, 1988.

A CIP catalogue record for this book
is available from the British Library.

10 9 8 7 6 5 4 3 2 1

Printed in China

Orchard Books is a division of Hachette Children's Books,
an Hachette UK company.
www.hachette.co.uk

Princess Sleepyhead and the NIGHT-NIGHT BEAR

PETER BENTLY

LAURA ELLEN ANDERSON

ORCHARD

The Moon's in the Sky

and the kingdom's asleep.
The cows are all slumbering.
So are the sheep.
The ducks are tucked up
in the roots of the willow.
The rabbit is drowsily
nibbling his pillow.

All the king's horses
are snug in the stable.
His poodles are cuddled up
under the table.
The ladies-in-waiting
are all in their beds.
The guards have dozed off
with their caps on their heads.

The king's having dreams about driving a train.

The queen's having dreams
about chocolate (again).
The palace is silent.
The lights are all out.

BUT hold on
a moment! Who's up
and about?

"I CAN'T

GET TO SLEEP!"

Princess Sleepyhead said.

"I'm fed up with **tossing** and **turning** in bed.

I've tried dropping off on my **side** and my **tummy**.
I've tried **lying still** on my back, like a **mummy**.
I've tried **counting sheep**, but it's no use at all.
I've tried **counting** all of the **spots** on my wall,
I can't get to sleep. I simply can't do it.
So I'll stay up **all night**
and that's all there is to it!"

1 2 3

"TOO-WHIT did you say?
TOO-WHOO to you too,"
said Owl at the window.
"Good evening to you!
Are you still wide awake?
Well, that isn't right.
A princess," he said,
"should be sleeping at night."

"I'll fetch my three friends.
They will know what to do."
Then off fluttered Owl with
another "TOO-WHOO!"

MY DEN

I CAN'T SLEEP!

SOON AFTER, the princess heard three little knocks,
And in came the owl with a mouse and a fox.

Mouse said, "A good bit of running about
Is just what is needed to tire you out!"

First they played
hide-and-squeak,
followed by chase.

Then they had fun
in a wheelbarrow race.

"Now then," said Fox as they fell in a heap.
"You must be exhausted and ready for sleep."
"Oh, no," laughed the princess,
"I want to play more.
I'm even more wide awake
now than before!"

The princess sat down on the end of her bed and sighed, "Well, I'll stay up all night, like I said."

"Oho," chuckled Owl. "But please don't forget

I said I'd bring **three** friends. There's one to come yet.

I think I just heard him outside on the stair."

Then into the room stepped a big friendly . . .

...BEAR.

"My name is
BARTHOLOMEW BROWNFUR-BROWN.
I hear there's a princess who can't settle down.
Some people call me the Sleepytime Ted.
Perhaps I can help you?" the friendly bear said.

"Probably not,"
Princess Sleepyhead sighed.
"Mouse, Fox and Owl
have already tried."

"There's a princess who can't get to sleep in my book," said the bear. "Snuggle down while I just take a look."

The princess lay down and Bartholomew read

of a tiny pea
under a princess's bed
that kept her awake
all the night until dawn.

"How daft!" Princess Sleepyhead said with a yawn.

Bartholomew said,
"Shall I read you another?"
as he plumped up her pillows
and pulled up the cover.

She whispered "Yes, please,"
and he started to tell
of a princess who went to sleep
under a spell.

"She slept for a hundred long years, so they say.

Then a handsome young prince came and woke her one day."

Bartholomew tucked up the drowsy princess.

"Shall I finish the story?"

She murmured, "Oh yes! What woke her up?"

The bear said, "A kiss..."

". . . perhaps it was something a little like **this**."

THEN the bear
and his friends whispered,
"Night-night. Sleep tight!"

As they slipped from
her bedroom and
into the night.

The End . . .